I Like Myself !!!

Lucylu and Gigi

Book 1

Story
by
Audrey Kharem, Ph.D.

I Like Myself
Lucylu & Gigi book 1
Published by Noble Strength Publishing
140 Roosevelt Ave, State College PA, 16801
Created 2012 by Audrey E. Kharem
Copyright © 2016 by Audrey E. Kharem
Illustrations by Andika Rodriguez

This is Alanna.
Her grandmother
calls her
Lucylu.

This is Grandmother. Alanna calls her Gigi.

Gigi, guess what?
I like myself !

How about you?

Oh yes, baby girl
I sure do!

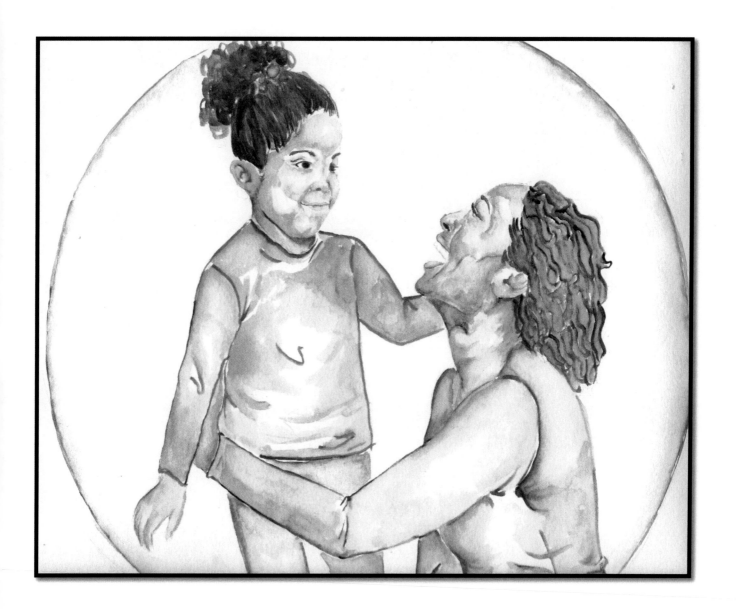

*Lucylu, I am glad that
you like yourself.*

*Liking yourself first, helps
you to like everyone else.*

*Now, tell me what it is that
you like about you,
because that's
important too.*

Gigi, I like that I can tie my shoes.

Criss cross, under the bridge, wrap around and pull the bow through.

That's how I learned to tie my shoes.

Gigi, I like that I can
write my name
and
I'm learning
how to read
books.

I like stories about animals and fairies and books that can teach me how to cook.

Gigi, I like the way
Mommy fixes my hair.

She brushes and brushes
and my hair stays curly
just how I like it,
so I don't care!

Gigi, I like that my body is strong.

I can jump high and run very fast.

I like that I am the tallest girl in my class.

Gigi, I like my smooth
brown skin.

It always feels
nice and soft.

I'm glad that when I
take a bath the brown
doesn't wash off!

*Gigi, when I look in
the mirror,
I like what I see.*

*I like the smile
that's smiling back
at me !*

Gigi, I like myself,
I like my friends
and
my toys too.

But Gigi, I really,
really
love you!

Well, thank you
baby girl.

You know I really,
really love you
too,
my Lucylu !

♫ Lucylu's Song

I like myself

I like myself

Cuz I'm so smart

And

I'm so cool   ♫

And

♫ I like you too

I'm Lucylu

If you want to learn how to sing Lucylu's song go to the website,
www.noblestrengthpublishing.com .

Made in the USA
Columbia, SC
06 July 2019